A Beginning-to-Read Book

W9-AAH-895

Dear Dragon's Colors 1,2,3

by Margaret Hillert

Illustrated by David Schimmell

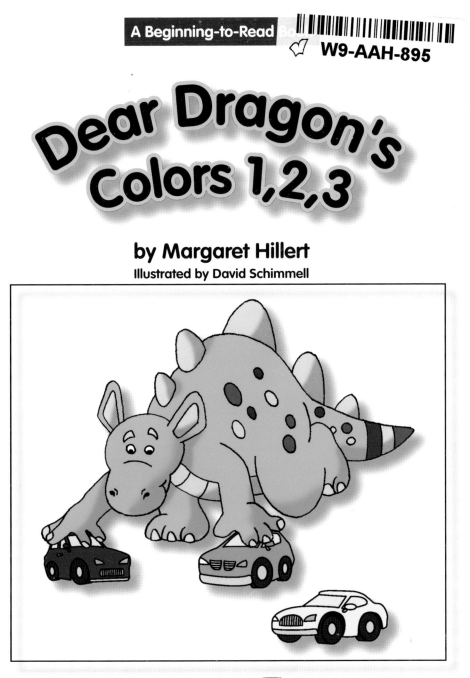

NORWOOD HOUSE PRESS

The **Dear Dragon** series is comprised of carefully written books that extend the collection of classic readers you may remember from your own childhood. Each book features text focused on common sight words. Through the use of controlled text, these books provide young children with abundant practice recognizing the words that appear most frequently in written text. Rapid recognition of high-frequency words is one of the keys for developing automaticity which, in turn, promotes accuracy and rate necessary for fluent reading. The many additional details in the pictures enhance the story and offer opportunities for students to expand oral language and develop comprehension.

Shannon Cannon

Shannon Cannon,
Literacy Consultant

Norwood House Press • P.O. Box 316598 • Chicago, Illinois 60631
For more information about Norwood House Press please visit our website at
www.norwoodhousepress.com or call 866-565-2900.

Paperback ISBN: 978-1-60357-100-5

The Library of Congress has cataloged the original hardcover edition with the following call number: 2010007370

Manufactured in the United States of America in North Mankato, Minnesota
197N—012012

Play with me.
Come play with me.
I like to play with cars.

1 little **red** car.
It can go, go, go.
It is fun to play with
a little **red** car.

1 little **red** car.

I have **2** little **blue** cars.
I can make them go up and
down.

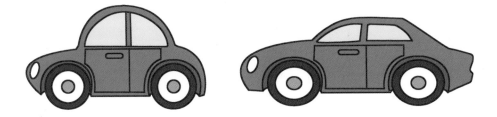

2 little **blue** cars.

I have **3** little **yellow** cars.
Yellow cars are pretty.
They can go in and out.

3 little **yellow** cars.

I have **4** little **green** cars.
Green is good.
I like **green**.

4 little **green** cars.

I have **5** little **orange** cars.
Oh, oh, oh.
What is this?
This is not good.

5 little **orange** cars.

I have **6** little **brown** cars.
Go, cars. Go.
This is fun, fun, fun.

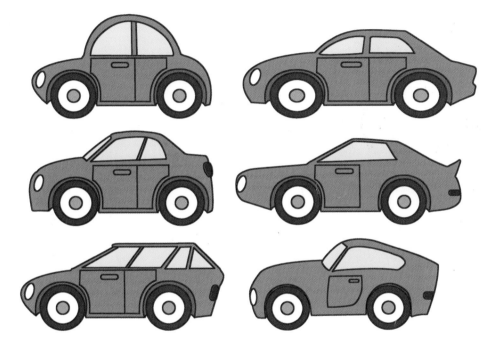

6 little **brown** cars.

I have **7** little **purple** cars.
Mother likes **purple**.
I like **purple**, too.

7 little **purple** cars.

I have **8** little **pink** cars.
How pretty.
Pink, pink, pink.

8 little **pink** cars.

I have **9** little **black** cars.
This is good.

9 little **black** cars.

I have **10** little **white** cars.
We can have fun with the cars.

10 little **white** cars.

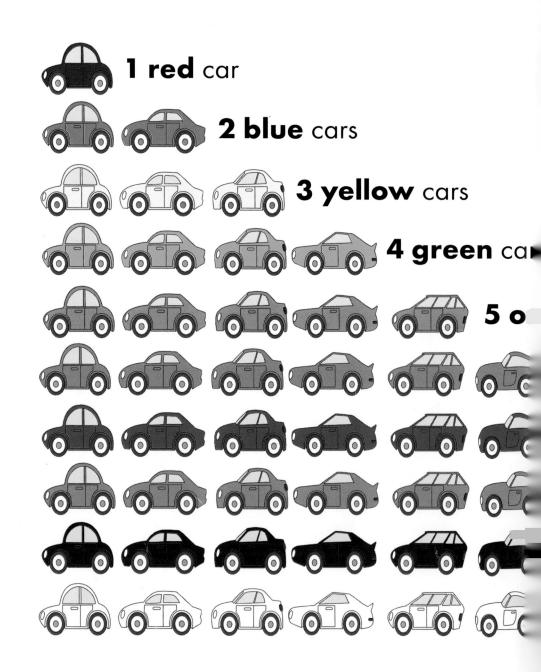

1 red car

2 blue cars

3 yellow cars

4 green ca

5 o

e cars

brown cars

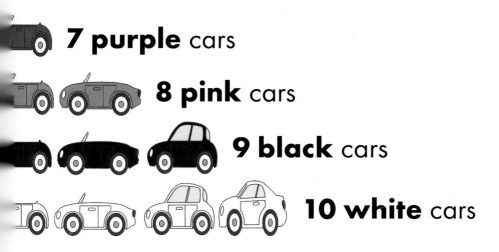

7 purple cars

8 pink cars

9 black cars

10 white cars

Wow!
Look at this.
So many cars.
So many, many cars.

Here you are with me.
And here I am with you.
What fun.
What fun, dear dragon.

WORD LIST

Dear Dragon's Colors 1,2,3 **uses the 56 pre-primer vocabulary words listed below**. This list can be used to practice reading the words that appear in the text. You may wish to write the words on index cards and use them to help your child build automatic word recognition. Regular practice with these words will enhance your child's fluency in reading connected text.

a	fun	look	red	wow
am				
and	go	make	so	yellow
are	good	many		you
at	green	me	the	
		Mother	them	
black	have		they	
blue	here	not	this	
brown	how		to	
		oh	too	
can	I	orange		
car(s)	in	out	up	
come	is			
	it	pink	we	
dear		play	what	
down	like(s)	pretty	white	
dragon	little	purple	with	

Photograph by Glenna Washburn

ABOUT THE AUTHOR

Margaret Hillert has written over 80 books for children who are just learning to read. Her books have been translated into many different languages and over a million children throughout the world have read her books. She first started writing poetry as a child and has continued to write for children and adults throughout her life. A first grade teacher for 34 years, Margaret is now retired from teaching and lives in Michigan where she likes to write, take walks in the morning, and care for her three cats.

ABOUT THE ADVISER

Shannon Cannon contributed the activities pages that appear in this book. Shannon serves as a literacy consultant and provides staff development to help improve reading instruction. She is a frequent presenter at educational conferences and workshops. Prior to this she worked as an elementary school teacher and as president of a curriculum publishing company.

ABOUT THE ILLUSTRATOR

David Schimmell served as a professional firefighter for 23 years before hanging up his boots and helmet to devote himself to working as an illustrator of children's books. David has happily created illustrations for the New Dear Dragon books as well as the artwork for educational and retail book projects. Born and raised in Evansville, Indiana, he lives there today with his wife and family.